LYNNLY LABOVITZ

## ABOUT THE AUTHOR

MIRIAM ENGELBERG is the author of *Planet 501c3: Tales from the Nonprofit Galaxy* and *Tantrum Comics.* Her work has been published in the *San Francisco Bay Guardian*, *Nonprofit Quarterly*, and CASE's *Currents* magazine. She lives in San Francisco with her husband and son.

# CANCER MADE ME A SHALLOWER PERSON

# CANCER

# MADE ME A SHALLOWER PERSON

## A MEMOIR IN COMICS

### MIRIAM ENGELBERG

Harper

*An Imprint of HarperCollinsPublishers*

CANCER MADE ME A SHALLOWER PERSON. Copyright © 2006 by Miriam Engelberg. All rights reserved. Printed in the United States of America. No part of this book may be used or reproduced in any manner whatsoever without written permission except in the case of brief quotations embodied in critical articles and reviews. For information address HarperCollins Publishers, 10 East 53rd Street, New York, NY 10022.

HarperCollins books may be purchased for educational, business, or sales promotional use. For information please write: Special Markets Department, HarperCollins Publishers, 10 East 53rd Street, New York, NY 10022.

FIRST EDITION

*Designed by Elliott Beard*

Library of Congress Cataloging-in-Publication Data

Engelberg, Miriam.
Cancer made me a shallower person : a memoir in comics / Miriam Engelberg.—
1st ed.
p.   cm.
ISBN-10: 0-06-078973-5
ISBN-13: 978-0-06-078973-2
1. Engelberg, Miriam—Comic books, strips, etc.  2. Breast—Cancer—Patients—United States—Biography.  3. Cartoonists—United States—Biography.  I. Title.
RC280.B8E57   2006
362.196'994490092—dc22                                    2005055141

06 07 08 09 10   ID/RRD   10 9 8 7 6 5 4 3 2 1

TO JIM AND AARON

# CONTENTS

# INTRODUCTION

From childhood I'd always planned to be a writer. Though I did manage to write a few short stories, I hit a wall when I attempted a novel. So many words! So many chapters! I'd mapped out the plot, but then I realized that for each plot point I had to actually create descriptions and conversations. Around this time, the form of the autobiographical monologue became popular, starting with Spalding Gray's *Swimming to Cambodia*. I scrapped the novel and wrote a monologue called "Interruptions," about how my family spent a lot of time trying to avoid getting sick (my parents boiled the dishes of sick family members to avoid the spread of colds and flu), but as an adult I realized that I actually enjoyed the time-out from regular life that a cold provided. For a few years I wrote and performed a number of monologues at small theaters in San Francisco. Eventually, I teamed up with a friend, Gayle Schmitt, and we wrote and performed a play about our experiences teaching (she had been teaching elementary school and I had been teaching high school) called *Spit Out Your Gun: It's School Policy*.

*Introduction*

When my husband and I decided to have a baby, I looked forward to mellowing out. Though I loved doing theater, it was a lot of work—not so much the performing part as the fact that we were doing our own producing and marketing. I pictured myself walking in the park with the baby, finally getting a chance to smell the roses so to speak. Most other parents told us how much fun parenting was. So my husband and I were completely unprepared for the tedium and exhaustion of taking care of a baby. We loved Aaron very much, of course, but we decided that there was a conspiracy among parents not to reveal the truth in order to lure unsuspecting couples into joining them. Or perhaps some people were better suited to the busy and chaotic life of baby-care. In any case, on the days when I was on duty at home (my husband and I took turns, since we both worked part-time) I began to long for some kind of creative project that I could work on.

One day I heard an NPR interview with Peter Kuper about his early autobiographical comics. It intrigued me so much that I ran straight down to my local comic bookstore, Comix Experience, to buy Peter Kuper comics. I immediately read his books with great enthusiasm; I've always enjoyed memoirs, but there was something about the way Kuper turned moments from his life into cartoons that I found both hilarious and touching. He wasn't afraid to laugh at his own foibles, and the self-deprecating tone struck a chord with me. I'd always enjoyed cartoons—as a child I read *Mad Magazine* voraciously—but Kuper showed me that cartoons could be a literary form as well.

From there I discovered lots of other autobiographical comics—

Harvey Pekar, Aline Kominsky-Crumb, Mary Fleener, and Lynda Barry, among others. I decided to try creating some comics about parenthood. With Harvey Pekar as my inspiration (he hires different artists to draw his comics), I mapped out my first set of panels and handed them to a friend who was eager to illustrate them. It never occurred to me to do the drawings, as I didn't consider myself an artist. We turned out to be bad collaborators; she changed my words, and despite her artistic skill, the look of the characters just didn't fit the vision I'd had. So I decided to do the drawings myself. Whenever Aaron took a nap, I immediately pulled out a notebook and worked on my comics. I discovered that for me, the writing and illustrating went together. I remembered as a child how much I'd enjoyed doing artwork, and couldn't believe I'd stopped for so many years.

Meanwhile, I continued working part-time at my day job as a computer trainer at CompassPoint Nonprofit Services. It turned out that Jan Masaoka, the executive director, loved comics. She asked me to create a few cartoons about the nonprofit sector, which we posted on our Web site, and this was the beginning of *Planet 501c3*, a monthly strip that soon developed a following among staff members at nonprofits all over the world. (Granted, the genre of nonprofit humor didn't have much competition!) CompassPoint added Chief Cartoonist to my title; I felt extremely lucky to have a job where I was paid to create cartoons. *Planet 501c3* cartoons are now also featured in a couple of books—the second edition of *Strategic Planning for Nonprofit Organizations* and a book for nonprofit IT staff called *The Accidental Techie*.

In the fall of 2001 I was diagnosed with breast cancer. I was forty-three. Aaron was only four years old. After weathering the initial shock, I began creating cartoons about having cancer. (I actually created the first cartoon while waiting for the biopsy, before I knew for sure that the tumor was malignant.) They say hardship reveals one's true character, and it was clear right away that I wouldn't be the heroic type of cancer patient portrayed in so many television shows and movies. My immediate response was to spend a lot of time in front of the television. I didn't go inward, I looked for pop culture distraction.

Years ago I'd performed "Interruptions," about taking a break from regular life while having a cold, but I hadn't counted on the degree of interruption provided by cancer. What is the point of life when illness takes over and becomes the main event? When someone goes through hard times, friends will say, "You can get through this." This implies a temporary state, like a Lifetime made-for-TV movie scenario, where the heroine comes out stronger in the end. At the beginning of my relationship with cancer, I too viewed it as something temporary. I had no idea that it would become a constant presence. I've always had a preoccupation with figuring out the point of life. When I was young I pictured intellectual achievement as my reason for being. (Can you tell my father was a professor?) Later, when I realized I wasn't interested in an academic path, I decided to go for the enjoyment factor instead—finding a nonacademic job I liked, hanging out with friends and family, playing and listening to music. . . . But faced with cancer and cancer treatments, it's hard to see life in terms of good times.

There are some days when I've literally lain in bed all day, in complete despair about my cancer, and watched bad science fiction movies on TV. But most of the time, drawing comics has been my lifeline through this cancer experience (that—and wanting to stay alive as long as possible for my husband and son, of course). We all have issues that follow us through life, no matter how much therapy we've had. The big one for me is about feeling different and alone—isolated in a state of Miriam-ness that no one else experiences. That's what drew me to read autobiographical comics, and that's why I hope my comics can be of comfort to other readers who might be struggling with issues similar to mine. When I was first diagnosed, I felt pressure to become someone different—someone nobler and more courageous than I was. But maybe nobility and courage aren't the only approaches to life with an illness; maybe the path of shallowness deserves more attention!

Life, death, enjoyment, and suffering . . . as I get older I feel more uncertain than ever about the point of it all. Maybe someday I'll have something profound to say about these important issues, but right now I have to go—it's time to watch *Celebrity Poker*.

CANCER MADE ME A SHALLOWER PERSON

# PERSONAL

END

# WAITING

# BIOPSY

# DIAGNOSIS

# BREAST CANCER AS A HOBBY

# CROSSWORDS

# LUCK

IN ANY CASE, I'M TIRED OF MY PARANOIA.
OW
A PAPER CUT! THAT'S A BAD SIGN ABOUT MY DAY.
AND I GOT IT FROM SEALING THIS ENVELOPE OF CARTOONS I'M SENDING TO AN EDITOR.
MAYBE IT MEANS THE MAGAZINE WON'T TAKE THEM.
I'M READY TO CHANGE MY ATTITUDE...
IT'S ALL GOOD.
WHOOSH
...BUT I CAN'T SEEM TO DO IT.
WAIT A MINUTE— NO ONE AROUND ME GOT SPLASHED. THE UNIVERSE HAS IT IN FOR ME - I KNEW IT!
MAYBE LUCK IS ALL ABOUT TEMPERAMENT...
...THEN I LOST MY JOB AND BROKE MY LEG, HA HA! LIFE'S SUCH AN ADVENTURE!
...AND SOME PEOPLE GET ALL THE LUCK.
END

# EMBARRASSMENT VS. DEATH

## ACE BANDAGE

# THE DISPOSITION OF DOCTORS

# HAIR

# THE F.O.L. GENE

# NAUSEA

...THEN ON DECEMBER 10TH I WORKED ON THAT DATABASE FOR,...OR WAS THAT ON THE 11TH? SORRY, I'M NOT BEING VERY COHESIVE TODAY.
COHESIVE? COHESIVE? IS THAT WHAT I WANTED TO SAY? COHE... YEAH, I GUESS THAT'S RIGHT.
STILL HAD MY HAIR — HAD ALREADY LOST MY MIND.
MY SISTER HAD PROMISED MY SON A LAVA LAMP FOR CHRISTMAS. THE ONE SHE BOUGHT WAS DARK RED WITH A PURPLE TINGE.
AARON—THIS WAS THE ONLY COLOR THEY HAD LEFT.
I LOVE IT!
SINCE STARTING CHEMO I HAD TURNED THE LIVING ROOM INTO MY BEDROOM. THE LAVA LAMP SAT ON THE TABLE BY THE WINDOWS.
AARON KEPT THE LAMP ON WHENEVER HE WAS IN THE ROOM. FROM MY POSITION ON THE FUTON, I COULDN'T HELP BUT NOTICE IT.
BLIND DATE
THE REDDISH-PURPLISH BLOBS MOVING IN SLOW MOTION THROUGH THE DARK RED LIQUID MADE ME FEEL I WAS LOOKING AT MY OWN LIVER AND KIDNEYS, FILLED WITH THE RED ADRIAMYCIN FROM MY LAST INFUSION OF CHEMO.

# SOMETHING UNPLEASANT AND YOU

# KEEPING UP WITH THE JONESES

# HANGNAIL

# STRESS

# SPIRITUALITY

WHEN I WAS YOUNG I RECKLESSLY PURSUED ENLIGHTENMENT AS IF THERE WERE NO TOMORROW...
WANT TO JOIN US FOR SOME VIPASSANA MEDITATION?
HMM- I DON'T THINK THAT WILL MIX WELL WITH MY IGNATIAN PRAYER PRACTICE... OH, I CAN'T RESIST- OK!
AT FIRST IT WAS GREAT...
EVERYTHING IN MY LIFE IS THE WAY IT'S SUPPOSED TO BE... WHOA! WHERE DID THAT COME FROM?
BUT AS THE YEARS WENT BY, THE REVELATIONS SLOWED DOWN AND THEN STOPPED COMPLETELY.
COME ON, COME ON... I'M GETTING NOTHING HERE!
OVER TIME I STOPPED PRAYING.
I KNOW YOU'RE YOUNG AND ENTHUSIASTIC. YOU THINK THIS WILL NEVER HAPPEN TO YOU. BUT LISTEN...
DON'T DO THINGS IN THE WRONG ORDER! SAVE YOUR AWAKENINGS FOR LATER IN LIFE WHEN YOU'LL REALLY NEED THEM.
WRONG:
AGE 21
...AND THEN DURING PRAYER I REALIZED I DON'T HAVE TO OBSESS OVER ROGER'S OPINION OF ME ANYMORE!
THAT'S GREAT!
RIGHT:
WANT TO COME WITH ME TO THE PASSOVER SEDER?
NAH- I'M GOING TO A PARTY WHERE I'LL DRINK TOO MUCH BEFORE ENGAGING IN MEANINGLESS SEX.

THAT'S WHEN I DECIDED TO MAKE CARTOONING MY SPIRITUAL PRACTICE. I GO TO A CAFE EVERY DAY AND DRAW FOR 30 MINUTES.
SESAME BAGEL WITH BUTTER.
I'M STILL NOSTALGIC FOR THOSE DAYS WHEN I THOUGHT I WAS GETTING CLOSER AND CLOSER TO ENLIGHTENMENT.
BUT MAYBE ENLIGHTENMENT'S NOT ALL IT'S CRACKED UP TO BE.
END

# THE CHEERFUL TECH

# TELEMARKETERS

# COMPASSION FATIGUE

# HILARIOUS NEVER BEFORE HEARD JOKES

# WEIGHT

NOW I WAS IN A SIMILAR STATE OF DENIAL ABOUT MY APPEARANCE.
WHO'S THAT PLUMP MIDDLE-AGED WOMAN IN THE WINDOW?
BUT THEN AGAIN, I'VE NEVER COMPLETELY ACCEPTED ADULTHOOD. IN MY MIND I'M STUCK SOMEWHERE IN MY 20S.
THIS "FELICITY" EPISODE IS RIVETING! WILL SHE GO FOR PRE-MED OR SWITCH TO ART?
INWARDLY, I'M STILL THE SAME PERSON I WAS 25 YEARS AGO.
THIS PHILOSOPHY CLASS IS CHANGING MY LIFE!
SO TRUE!
KANT
KANT
OR IS THAT JUST ANOTHER MISPERCEPTION?
THIS PHILOSOPHY CLASS IS CHANGING MY LIFE!
I DOUBT IT.
KANT
TV GUIDE
LUCKILY, CARTOONING FORCES ME TO GET HONEST ABOUT WHO I REALLY AM.
OVER 5' TALL
ONLY HAS KIND THOUGHTS ABOUT OTHERS.
I HAVE A DUTY TO PORTRAY MYSELF AS REALISTICALLY AS POSSIBLE!
TINY WAIST
NEVER CHOOSES "PEOPLE" MAGAZINE OVER "THE NEW YORKER".
END

WE INTERRUPT THESE PHILOSOPHICAL MUSINGS WITH AN INVITATION TO HAWAII...
FORMER CO-WORKER, NOW A PROPERTY MANAGER ON MAUI.
...AND THE OWNERS SAID YOU CAN STAY IN THE GUESTHOUSE.
I LEFT JIM AND AARON AT HOME AND SET OFF FOR A RESTFUL WEEK IN HAWAII. IN BETWEEN SWIMMING AND READING TRASH BOOKS BY THE POOL, I WATCHED CABLE TV IN MY ROOM.
NOW THAT YOU'VE OVERCOME BULIMIA AND A DRUG HABIT YOU CAN FOCUS ON TRAPPING THAT STALKER!
HMM, I THINK I'VE SEEN THIS LIFETIME MOVIE ALREADY. OR DID I?
YES, BUT FIRST I NEED TO PROVE THAT MY HUSBAND POISONED HIS FIRST WIFE.
I'D BEEN WONDERING FOR AWHILE WHETHER WATCHING PORN COULD JUMP-START MY LIBIDO. THE CABLE GUIDE LISTED AN ADULT CHANNEL, SO I GAVE IT A TRY.
AWW MAN— IT'S SCRAMBLED!
STILL, A LITTLE OF THE MOVIE MADE IT THROUGH.
MOAN
GASP
OH BABY
I HAD TO ADMIT IT WAS A TURN-ON, INTERMITTENTLY...
WHOA — LOOK AT THE SIZE OF... OH WAIT, THAT'S JUST AN ARM.

WHEN I GOT BACK TO SAN FRANCISCO I DECIDED TO RENT AN EROTIC MOVIE. I PICKED A QUIET TIME AT MY LOCAL VIDEO STORE AND PUSHED THE SWINGING RED DOORS INTO THE ADULT AREA.

BEING IN A ROOM FILLED WITH PORN WAS OVERWHELMING, ESPECIALLY WHEN ALL THE MOVIES SEEMED AIMED AT MEN...

BREAST-ENHANCED VIXENS WITH GUYS LIKE YOU

WHEN A MAN CAME INTO THE AREA, I HURRIEDLY LEFT. THAT'S WHEN I SPOTTED A SOFT-CORE SECTION OUT IN THE REGULAR STORE.

HMM—"EMMANUELLE"!

"EMMANUELLE" WAS A CLASSIC—WHEN I WAS IN COLLEGE IT PLAYED AT THE UNIVERSITY CINEMA. SOME GUYS FROM MY DORM WENT TO SEE IT AND CAME BACK SEMI-TRAUMATIZED.

IT WAS INTENSE!

IT FREAKED ME OUT, MAN.

BUT WHEN JIM AND I STARTED WATCHING, WE GOT BORED PRETTY QUICKLY. FOR ONE THING, THERE WAS A LOT OF DUBBED 1970s-STYLE DIALOGUE...

YOU ARE NOT MY PLAYTHING AND YOU ARE NOT MY BEAUTY— YOU ARE BEAUTY.

CAN THIS... BE LOVE?

...AND THE SEX SCENES ALL ENDED JUST AS THINGS WERE GETTING INTERESTING...

LET'S FAST-FORWARD TO A SEX SCENE.

THIS IS A SEX SCENE.

# EARPLUGS

# 5 EZ STEPS

END

# FAMILY HISTORY

# JUDGMENT

# THE UNDEAD

...WHEN SUDDENLY I BECAME THE UNDEAD.
GLUG
GURGLE
SOCIAL NICETIES ARE NEVER QUITE THE SAME AFTER YOU'VE HAD CANCER.
PIERCING, CONCERNED LOOK.
UM...
HOW ARE YOU?
SOMETIMES I'M JUST NOT IN THE MOOD TO GET INTO IT, SO I PRETEND TO MISS THE SUBTEXT.
FINE! HOW ARE YOU?
BUT OTHER TIMES I ANSWER MORE HONESTLY.
I'M OK... I HOPE... KNOCK ON WOOD...
WE INTERRUPT THIS CARTOON WITH BREAKING NEWS...
THE DAY BEFORE A ROUTINE DOCTOR'S APPOINTMENT, I WAS CALMLY WORKING ON THIS PIECE.
IT'S FUNNY HOW OVERLY CONCERNED EVERYONE GETS.
CHUCKLE!

# A POTPOURRI OF SCANS

## INFOMERCIAL

# VALIUM IN THE WORKPLACE

MY APPROACH TO HARDSHIP IS A TAD DIFFERENT.
WHAT? WE HAVE TO HIKE ANOTHER MILE? AND THERE ARE NO BATHROOMS AT THE CAMPSITE? THIS IS UNBEARABLE!
IT TAKES A SPECIAL GIFT TO LIVE IN THE MOMENT WITH NO PERSPECTIVE WHATSOEVER.
DON'T WORRY- AT 3 MONTHS HE'LL START SLEEPING BETTER AND YOU'LL GET SOME REST.
3 WHOLE MONTHS? THIS IS UN-BEARABLE!
WAAH WAAH WAAH
BUT WHO'S TO SAY THAT ONE APPROACH IS BETTER THAN ANOTHER? HIS WAY...
WELL, OLD BOY, I BELIEVE THAT'S CHECK MATE!
HOW ABOUT WE MAS-TICATE A NEW SET AND PLAY AGAIN?
... OR MY WAY?
WELL, OLD GIRL, I BELIEVE THAT'S CHECK-MATE!
WE'RE ALL GOING TO DIE! AAAAH!
IN ANY CASE, CANCER'S A WHOLE DIFFERENT THING. I'D LIKE TO SEE MR.-STIFF-UPPER-LIP HANDLE THAT!
THE INFUSION TAKES AN HOUR? JOLLY GOOD. ANYONE CARE FOR A GAME OF CHESS?

END

# NEW REVELATION

# PAUL'S VISUALIZATION

# THE ULTIMATE HYPNOTHERAPY

# BRAIN RADIATION

# HIT BY A BUS

# HYPOCHONDRIA OR INTUITION?

# SURVIVOR

# FAMILY MELANCHOLY

EXACTLY!
I'VE TRIED TO GLOM ON TO OTHER PEOPLE'S BELIEFS...
TELL ME AGAIN ABOUT SENSING YOUR DEAD BROTHER'S PRESENCE.
WAIT A MINUTE- YOU'RE JUST USING ME FOR MY BELIEF IN AN AFTERLIFE, AREN'T YOU?!
BUT MOSTLY I'VE CULTIVATED A PRACTICE CALLED "AVOIDANCE."
UH OH- THOUGHTS OF DEATH COMING ON. QUICK- TURN ON MATLOCK!
BACK IN THE DAYS WHEN I MEDITATED, I DID HAVE AN "AHA" EXPERIENCE ON THE 51 BUS IN OAKLAND.
ONCE WE'RE CREATED, NOTHING CAN DESTROY OUR ESSENCE.
WOW!
OVER THE YEARS I'VE OFTEN SPOKEN OF THAT INSIGHT.
(NOTE: PERSONAL "AHA" EXPERIENCES INCREDIBLY BORING TO OTHERS.)
...SO I'M ON THE 51 BUS AND I HAVE THIS REALIZATION- NOTHING CAN DESTROY OUR ESSENCE! ISN'T THAT WILD?!
UH HUH.
YAWN
IT'S GOOD TO HAVE SOMETHING COMFORTING TO HOLD ON TO WHEN TIMES GET ROUGH.
WHENEVER I'M AFRAID, I PICTURE GOD RIGHT THERE NEXT TO ME!
I PICTURE AN ABSTRACT INSIGHT ABOUT OUR ESSENCE.
SIGH
END

# HOW OLD IS OLD ENOUGH?

# YOU LOOK GOOD

# THE CANCER CHANNEL

# TEACHING HIGH SCHOOL VS. CANCER

# BITTERNESS AND ENVY

# IN PERSPECTIVE

# BREAST CANCER SUPPORT RESOURCES

Advocacy, Information, and Support

**The Breast Cancer Fund: www.breastcancerfund.org**

The Breast Cancer Fund

1388 Sutter Street, Suite 400

San Francisco, CA 94109-5400

Telephone: 415-346-8223

E-mail: info@breastcancerfund.org

**Breast Cancer Action: www.bcaction.org**

Breast Cancer Action

55 New Montgomery, Suite 323

San Francisco, CA 94105

Telephone: 1-877-2STOPBC (toll free)

E-mail: info@bcaction.org

**Susan B. Komen Foundation: www.komen.org**

> Susan B. Komen Foundation
>
> 5005 LBJ Freeway, Suite 250
>
> Dallas, TX 75244
>
> Breast Cancer Helpline: 1-800-462-9273 (toll free)
>
> Telephone: 972-855-1600
>
> Fax: 972-855-1605

**Breastcancer.org: www.breastcancer.org**

Includes information about research, prevention, symptoms, and treatment. Runs chat rooms for breast cancer patients.

**American Cancer Society: www.cancer.org**

Offers cancer information and runs a Cancer Survivors Network for support.

> Telephone: 1-800-ACS-2345 (or 1-866-228-4327 for TTY)
>
> E-mail via form on Web site.

**Celebrate Life International, Inc.: www.celebratelife.org**

A support site for African-American women with breast cancer.

> Celebrate Life International, Inc.
>
> 6060 Lake Acworth Drive, Suite N
>
> Acworth, GA 30101
>
> Telephone: 770-529-7700
>
> Fax: 770-529-7711
>
> E-mail: request-info@CelebrateLife.org

**KidsCope: www.kidscope.org**

A support site for children whose parent or guardian has been diagnosed with cancer.

E-mail via form on Web site.

**Breastlink: www.breastlink.com**

Updates on the latest research on breast cancer treatment.

E-mail via form on Web site.

**Young Survival Coalition: www.youngsurvival.org**

A site devoted to support younger women with breast cancer.

Young Survival Coalition

155 6th Avenue, 10th Floor

New York, NY 10013

Telephone: 212-206-6610

Fax: 212-807-7199

E-mail: info@youngsurvival.org

**People Living with Cancer: www.plwc.org**

A site run by the American Society of Clinical Oncology to help patients make informed health decisions.

> People Living with Cancer
>
> American Society of Clinical Oncology
>
> 1900 Duke Street, Suite 200
>
> Alexandria, VA 22314
>
> Telephone: 703-797-1914
>
> Fax: 703-299-1044
>
> E-mail: contactus@plwc.org

**Y-Me National Breast Cancer Organization: www.y-me.org**

Breast cancer information, plus a twenty-four-hour hotline for those diagnosed with breast cancer: 1-800-221-2141 (English) and 1-800-986-9505 (Español)

> Site also states that they have interpreters in 150 languages.
>
> Y-ME National Breast Cancer Organization
>
> 212 W. Van Buren, Suite 1000
>
> Chicago, IL 60607
>
> Telephone: 312-986-8338
>
> Fax: 312-294-8597

**CancerCare: www.cancercare.org**

A national organization that offers free professional support services online to cancer patients. Runs an online support group, among other programs.

Telephone: 1-800-813-HOPE

E-mail via form on Web site.

## CLINICAL TRIALS

Many breast cancer patients choose to enter a clinical trial, whereby they can receive new treatments not yet approved for general use.

**Breastcancertrials.org: www.breastcancertrials.org**

A service to match breast cancer patients to clinical trials in the San Francisco Bay Area and Sacramento.

**ClinicalTrials.gov: www.clinicaltrials.gov**

National search site for clinical trials (not just breast cancer).

## ALTERNATIVE MEDICINE

It's best to get information about alternative/complementary medicine from nonprofit organizations. Many for-profit Web sites offer information about products that are "proven" to be effective against cancer, but are actually just selling a product.

**Annie Appleseed Project: www.annieappleseedproject.org**
A nonprofit offering information about complementary, alternative medicine, vitamins, and nutrients, with links to other similar sites.

## BOOKS

New and informative books are coming out about breast cancer all the time. Here are three that are frequently read by women in my support group.

### *Dr. Susan Love's Breast Book* by Dr. Susan Love

Widely available, with new editions appearing at intervals. A very comprehensive and informative look at breast health issues, including breast cancer. You probably won't find a breast cancer patient who doesn't own this book!

### *The Red Devil: To Hell with Cancer—and Back* (sometimes under the subtitle *A Memoir About Beating the Odds*) by Katherine Russell Rich

A well-written, and funny, memoir about Katherine Russell Rich, who was diagnosed at thirty-two and has survived metastatic breast cancer for many years now.

***The Breast Cancer Survival Manual, Third Ed.: A Step-by-Step Guide for the Woman with Newly Diagnosed Breast Cancer***
**by John Link, M.D.**

When I was first diagnosed, Susan Love's book was somewhat overwhelming. My support group recommended this shorter guide, which was very helpful in the beginning.

MAGAZINES

*CURE: Cancer Updates, Research & Education*

www.curetoday.com

A free quarterly magazine (available both online and in hard copy) that provides scientific information in easy-to-understand language with equally understandable illustrations.

*MAMM: Women, Cancer, and Community*

www.mamm.com

A magazine started in 1997 that is devoted to delivering information for women diagnosed with breast or reproductive cancer.

# ACKNOWLEDGMENTS

I have to start, of course, by thanking my wonderful, loving husband, Jim, and our son, Aaron, who have had to endure not only my illness but also years of my leaving the house early to get my cartooning done before work. Aaron keeps me interested in the natural world—crystals and insects and animals—at a time when it's tempting to give up on the world and retreat completely into myself.

Many thanks to Wendy Sharp, Patti Breitman, and Carole Bidnick for putting me on the path to finding an agent, and to Irene Moore (before moving on to become a magazine editor), my original agent at Frederick Hill Bonnie Nadell, Inc., for believing so strongly in my book and finding a fantastic publisher for it. And a huge thanks to Gail Winston, my editor at HarperCollins, and Katherine Hill, Gail's assistant, who have been a delight to work with. Their incisive comments have made for a better book, and their supportive approach was just what I needed to finish this book in the midst of a cancer recurrence and chemo. I am also grateful to Bonnie Nadell, my current agent, for her invaluable help as the book goes into production.

This book wouldn't even exist without Gayle Schmitt, my best friend and muse. For years we've met for "art dates" to keep ourselves working on creative projects (she's a wonderful singer-songwriter). I can't thank her enough. I'm also indebted to my sister, Elise, for so much that I can't even list everything. I'm glad she decided to move to San Francisco many years ago! Thanks, too, to Matt Knoth, her partner, for his thoughtful gesture in buying me a PlayStation to keep me entertained during a difficult time (even though I lose every game pretty much instantly). I'm also grateful for Gayle's brother, Paul Schmitt, for his extensive help in commenting on cartoons and helping me put the book in order.

Thanks to my parents for their ongoing support, and for being such good sports when I put them in my cartoons!

Thanks to Dorene Paul, who taught me years ago not to let daily chores get in the way of my cartooning, to Mark Ziemann, my cartoon art teacher, who helped me find my style of drawing, to Bart Johnson for his continued belief in me and for introducing me to Lauren Weinstein, a great cartoonist, who took time out as her own book was going into production to help me out with all sorts of practical book advice.

Thanks to everyone who helped us pack up and move, and/or brought food over, and/or drove me to massive doctors' appointments when Jim was at work, and/or gave me technical help with the computer end of things, and more: Gayle and Paul (again!); Tom Drohan; Beverly Patterson; Deirdre Kennedy; Sue Bennett; Roald Alexander; Ralph Berger; Kathryn Hyde; Judy Goldstein; Kathy Hoegger; Paul Zeitz and Cathy Petrick (for years of politely laughing at my cartoons, plus some cartoon ideas); Linda and Bob Klett; Trish Strickland; Regina Brunig; Sherri Corron; Trish McGrath (thanks for the free massages!); Debbie Peterson; Wendy Sharp; Laura Vida; David Porter and his wife, Antigone; Karen Aitchison (who also helped me edit the original book proposal); Jack Hanken (for the CDs to keep my spirits up); Kathy Bristol (for the healing earrings); George and Harry for all the great flowers; Ambrosia for coming over to watch poker on TV with me; Wendy Ellen for keeping me entertained with DVD reviews; and Martha Keavney, whose cartoons always keep me laughing.

Many thanks and a heartfelt farewell to CompassPoint Nonprofit Services, my workplace for thirteen years. I think of CompassPoint as a community of friends more than a workplace, which is why it is so hard to leave. Thanks to Jan Masaoka, CompassPoint's executive director, for encouraging my cartooning and officially making me chief cartoonist as part of my job. CompassPoint stood behind me beyond the call of duty through two bouts of cancer.

What would I have done without the amazing women from my support groups? Thanks to all of you for sticking by me even when I didn't return calls, and to the Breast Health coordinators at Kaiser, Lori Ross and Elizabeth Barbieri, and support group leader Diane Scott at St. Mary's Hospital. And, of course, grateful thanks to the doctors and nurses who have cared for me—Dr. Brian Lewis, Dr. James Constant, Dr. Larry Margolis, Dr. Penny Sneed, and the fabulous oncology nurses, especially Ellie Cannon, who has put up with years of my nausea complaints and never once looked annoyed.

Finally, I would like to acknowledge two cafés where I did most of the work on this book—the Grove on Fillmore, which plays the best and most eclectic music I've ever heard in a café, and, most of all, Café Venue at Third and Market, where I used to go every day until the cancer recurred. The staff at Café Venue actually sent me flowers and a card when they heard about my illness. Thanks for all the cups of tea and friendly service!

There's no way I can mention every friend who has encouraged me over the years, or who has called or written in response to my illness. Just know that your love and concern has sustained me through so much. Thanks everyone!